MW00910654

This Book belongs to

....

FLY TRAP

(A CHILDREN'S STORY)

by

Eli Gurevich

Illustrations by Blueberry Illustrations

All rights reserved.

No part of this book may be used or reproduced in any manner without written permission from the copyright holder.

Printed in the United States of America.

Copyright © Eli Gurevich

ISBN: 978-0-578-31779-3

DEDICATION

Dedicated to my forever inspiration and my biggest flex, my daughter, Hannah, the fearless (aka Goose, aka Danger Mouse, aka Pink Lightning, aka HaHa). Sky's the limit for you, my warrior princess. Dance, sing, and laugh, all the way up.

This is a story about two best friends,
Who travel the world from end to end.

ichie and Marvin travel the planet, dining everywhere,
rom country barns to the finest restaurants in Manhattan.

They don't have a suitcase and don't need supplies,
Because Richie and Marvin are a pair of FLIES!

They live where they want, wherever there's food.
Sometimes a Chinese restaurant if they're in a fortune cookie mood.

THANK YOU

OURAGE IS DOING
AT YOU'RE AFRAID TO DO

They have a sweet tooth for sure,
So they're at the bakery sometimes.

Pastries are their favorite and they eat all that they want,
Never waiting on lines.

Such a happy life these little bugs live,
These two best of friends,
Live how they want,
It all depends.
If there's food, they'll stay,

If not, they'll go.
They love warm weather,
They hate the snow.

Now, it must have been summer, hot as it was,
It was a silent apartment except for their buzz.
Marvin and Richie had found a new home,
A dirty, empty, unkempt place, with no people, no phone.

Then the day came when a man showed up,

And then came more humans, who came to clean up.

So it seemed it was time to move out and give paradise up.

"Before we leave, let's see if he's clean."

"Maybe he's messy and we can all live together."

So they waited a while to see if life would get better.

And as they waited, they noticed a difference.
Living life messy seemed to be this human's preference.
They couldn't believe it, this was better than before,
What a slob he was, leaving food, dirt, and crumbs, from the doors to the doors.

He didn't clean and seemed not to care,

He was the flies' kind of guy! They Weren't Going Nowhere!

What a glorious life these flies were living,

Every day eating, sleeping, and singing.

Then one day a tragedy happened,

Marvin was starving, so while the human was napping,

Marvin flew down to eat some food left on a napkin.

Richie warned him to not get too close,

"Don't worry, he's sleeping, and that's *strawberry jam* on top

of that toast!"

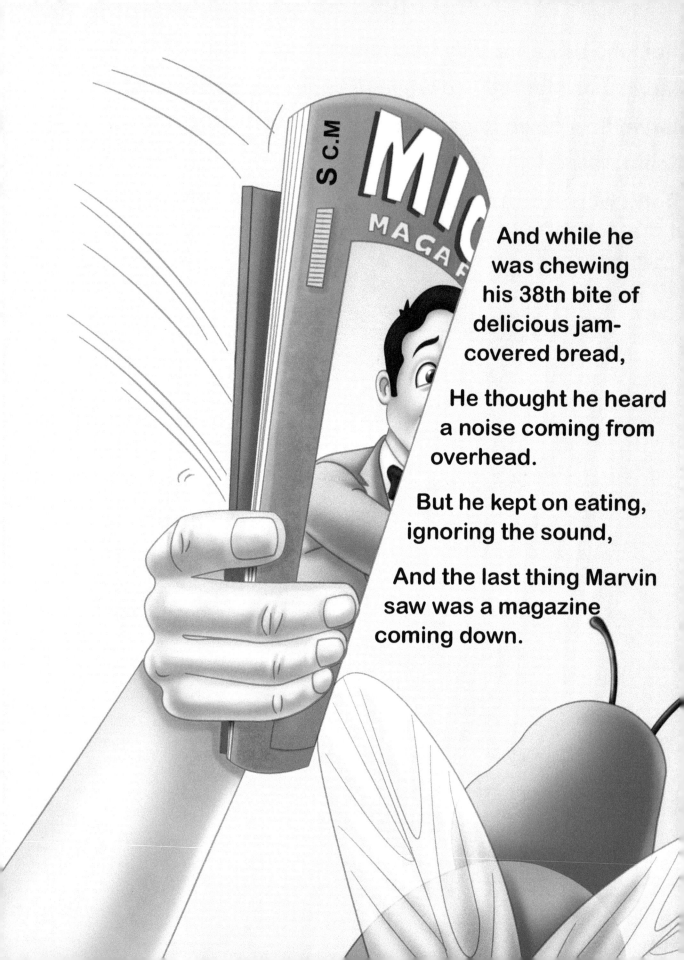

And while he was chewing his 38th bite of delicious jam-covered bread,

He thought he heard a noise coming from overhead.

But he kept on eating, ignoring the sound,

And the last thing Marvin saw was a magazine coming down.

NOOOOOOOOOOOOOOO!" screamed out Richie,

When he saw what had happened.

Marvin, wake up!"

But there was no reaction.

Now Richie was angry and vowed revenge.

"I will get even with him, I will avenge you, my friend!"

Then Richie let out a tremendous roar (at least for a fly),

He screamed, "This means war!"

Richie flew up and looked the man in his eyes,

"Mess with my family, prepare for revenge of the flies!"

So the battle begins,

Richie pulls out all of his tricks.

He studies his foe,

He is cunning and patient.

He plans his attacks carefully,

Waiting for the right opportunity.

And when it's time, he strikes,
In the middle of the night.
Without any fear,
While the man is sleeping,
Richie is buzzing in his ear.

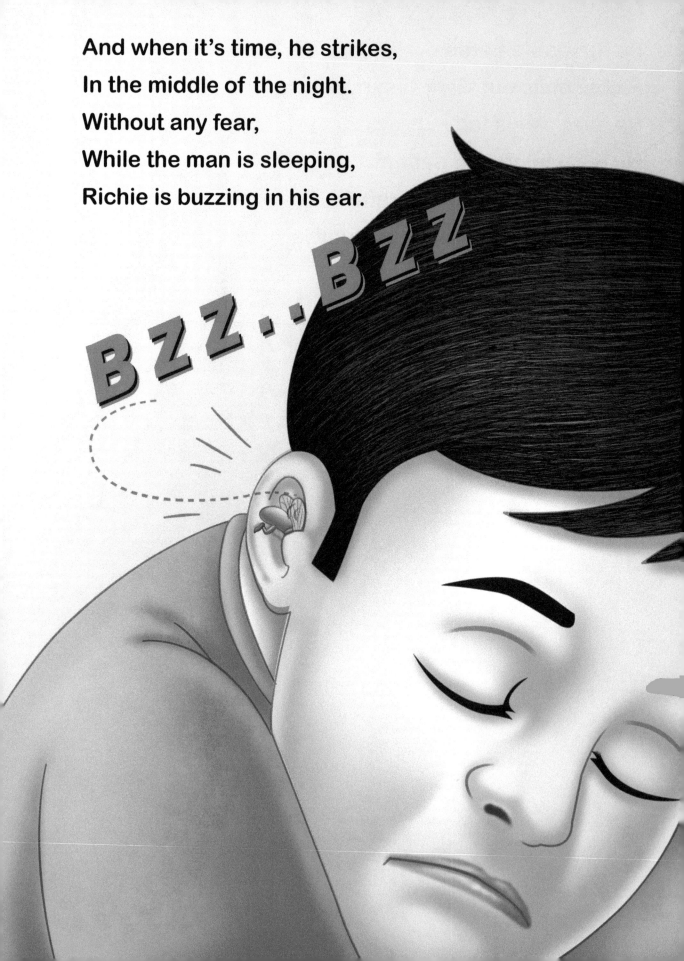

The man wakes up,

Away Richie goes,

When he's back asleep,

Richie goes "bzzz, bzzz" in the man's nose.

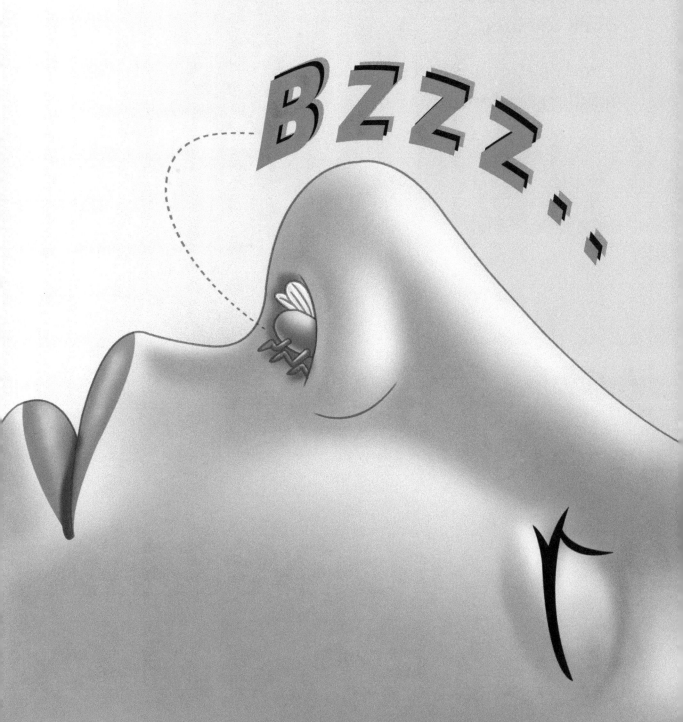

Again he wakes up,

And then just when he goes back to sleep,

There's Richie again, tickling his feet.

All night every night it is like this,

The man is getting no sleep and starts to get suspicious.

"Can it be that a fly is messing with me?

Impossible, no way! I must be crazy!"

But there he is again, right on top of his soup,
"Get out of here, Fly!" But the fly doesn't move.
"Are you the fly that keeps me up all night?"
No reply from the fly,
But the man sees something in its eyes,
That told him he was in for a fight.

So now the man understood that Richie didn't like him,
And that he was coming to get him. Imagine that, a fly
fighting!

Richie was ready,
And it was time for confrontation.
It wasn't just for Marvin anymore,
It was for the whole fly nation.

The man grabbed a magazine and waved it in the air,

Richie flew right up to him, the fly wasn't scared!

The man swung the magazine,

And missed Richie by a mile.

But he did manage to hit a lamp that came crashing down on the tile.

Again he swung, and again he missed,
Those crazy flies and their crazy tricks.
This time the stereo gave its last toot,
'Cause down it came crashing right on
his foot.

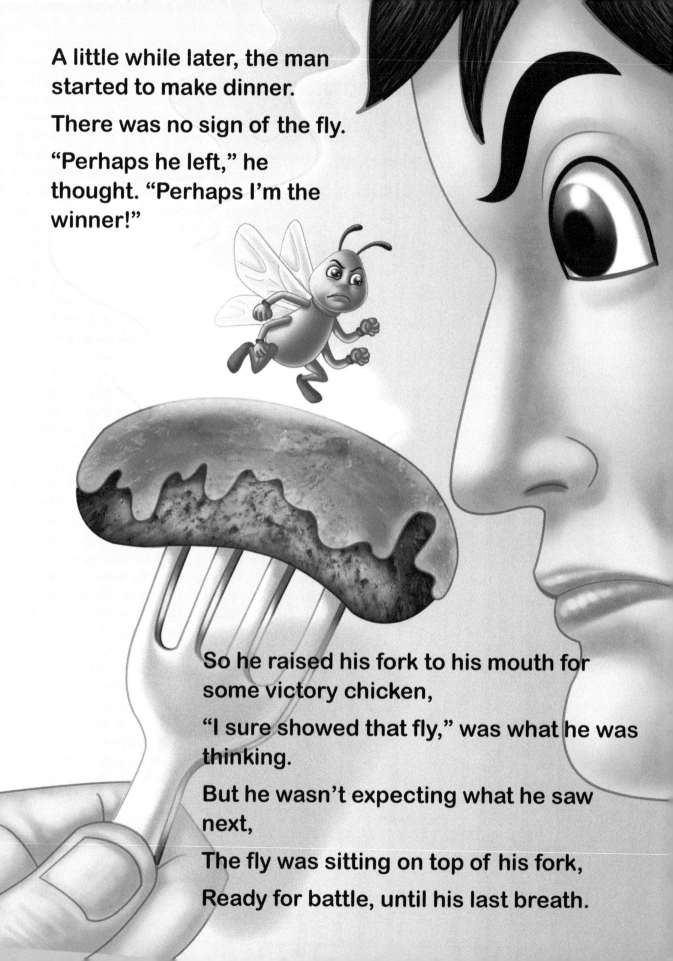

A little while later, the man started to make dinner.

There was no sign of the fly.

"Perhaps he left," he thought. "Perhaps I'm the winner!"

So he raised his fork to his mouth for some victory chicken,

"I sure showed that fly," was what he was thinking.

But he wasn't expecting what he saw next,

The fly was sitting on top of his fork,

Ready for battle, until his last breath.

He tries to catch him quick with his hand.

What a mistake!

On his pants,

Is where the hot chicken lands.

He's had enough of this battle scene,

He vows to smush this bug like he did the other with his magazine.

He flails his arms and swings his papers,

He misses by miles,

Richie's never been safer.

He swings and swings,
And misses and misses.
Soon there was food on the floor,
And more broken dishes.

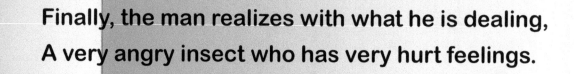

Finally, the man realizes with what he is dealing,
A very angry insect who has very hurt feelings.

So he leaves the house and he goes to the store,

He comes back with weapons—fly swatters, sprays, traps, and more!

Sticky yellow paper he hangs on the ceiling,

"The fly has emotions? Well, I too have feelings.

And my feelings believe

That it is either the fly or me.

We'll see who comes out of this victoriously."

Richie sees him,
And he is ready for this.
Here comes the swatter!
Another big miss!

The man takes out the spray,
And starts trying to use it.
But, alas, Richie's too fast,
Watching from another room in amusement.

Richie flies in, zooming with real haste,
He pokes the man in the eye,
Missing Richie, the man smacks his own face.

This time he falls,

Taking the television down with him.

A loud crash is heard, waking the landlord's children.

The sticky yellow paper falls right on his head,

The man starts yelling loudly,

"Come out, Fly! You heard what I said!"

Then from the door a knocking came,
The man got up with a look of shame.
He opened the door, and what did he see?

His neighbors and landlord looking very angry.
"What are you doing?" they angrily said.

"I'm trying to get rid of a fly," he replied.
"Looks like a fly's trying to get rid of you instead."

They were making jokes and laughing at him,
Until they saw the apartment,
And that was the end of their grins.
The landlord came in and saw the horror,
The apartment was trashed.

"This is what woke my two daughters!"
"It's the middle of the night,
And you broke everything in sight!"
The man tried to explain how the fly started it,
But the landlord and neighbors were believing none of it.

A couple of days later, and that was that,
The man was moving out, and as he looked back,
He saw the destruction from the fly's attack.
Then he said goodbye and closed the door,

Realizing he underestimated the fly, and so he lost the war.

The car sped off as Richie looked on,
The human versus the fly,
And the fly had won!

ABOUT THE AUTHOR

Eli Gurevich is a first-time author, a first-time father, and a first-time rabbit owner. Living in his hometown of New York City, he was inspired one day to write this children's story when he unexpectedly felt strange remorse for swatting a fly and wondering if flies have emotions. He's still not sure, but no longer swats flies.

CPSIA information can be obtained
at www.ICGtesting.com
Printed in the USA
LVHW070839070422
715600LV00002B/24

9 780578 3177

.